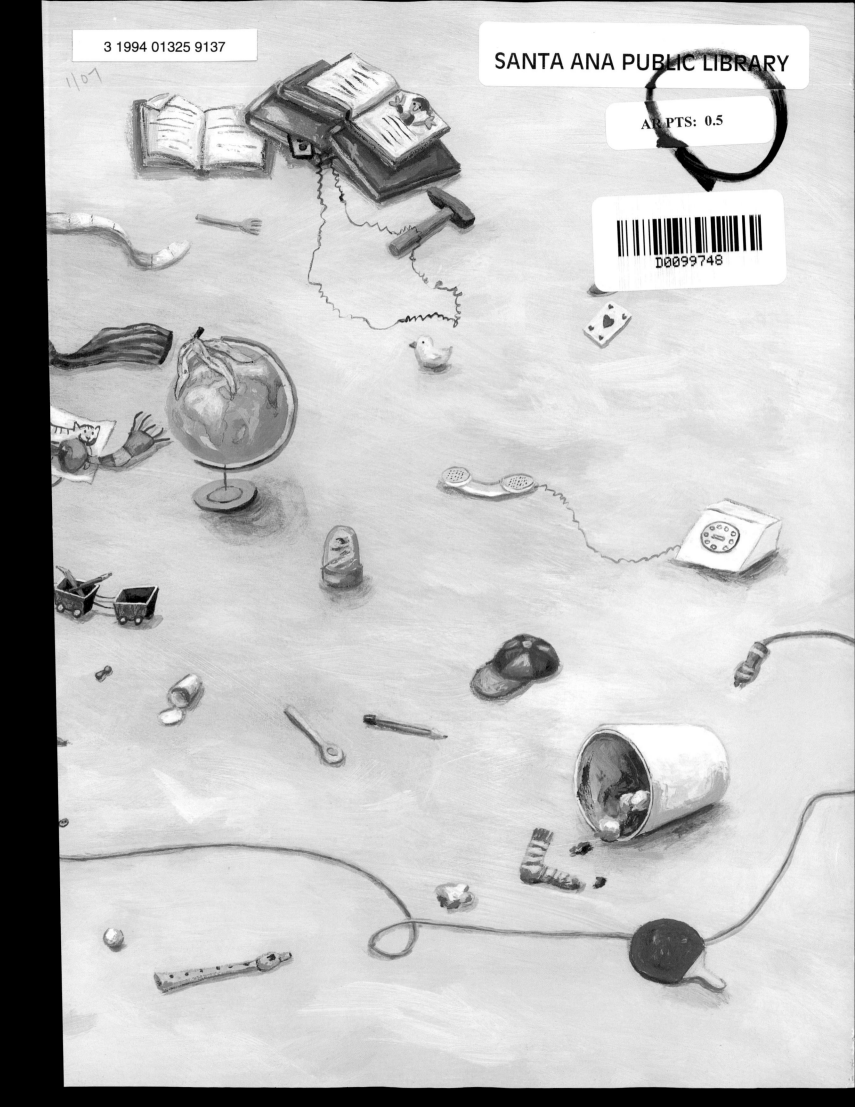

a minedition book
published by Penguin Young Readers Group

Text copyright © 2006 by Géraldine Elschner
Illustrations copyright © 2006 by Alexandra Junge
Original title: Schluss mit dem Chaos
Coproduction with Michael Neugebauer Publishing Ltd., Hong Kong.
Rights arranged with "minedition" Rights and Licensing AG, Zurich, Switzerland.

Published simultaneously in Canada.
Manufactured in Hong Kong by Wide World Ltd.
Typesetting in Veljovic book by Jovica Veljovic.
Color separation by Fotoreproduzioni Grafiche, Verona, Italy.

Library of Congress Cataloging-in-Publication Data available upon request.

ISBN 0-698-40047-X
10 9 8 7 6 5 4 3 2 1
First Impression

For more information please visit our website: www.minedition.com

# Mark's Messy Room

Géraldine Elschner

with pictures by

Alexandra Junge

translated by

Charise Myngheer

minedition

Carlo was one unhappy cat.
"I wonder how many other cats
have to sleep in a flower pot?"
he thought to himself.
"Ouch!" he meowed with resentment
when he bumped into the cactus for the
hundredth time.
"It's not safe to live here!"

Carlo wanted to curl up in his bed, but it was full of
Mark's toys. He was hungry, but his food smelled like
Mark's stinky socks.
"Lazy bum," thought Carlo as he made his way
through Mark's messy room.

Carlo knew that Mark was just a kid. And kids are supposed to be a little messy. But lately, things had gone too far. Mark hadn't cleaned his room for weeks!

"Enough is enough!" decided Carlo. "I don't want to live in this messy room anymore!  No one can make me!" And just like that, Carlo left.

At first,
running through the streets was fun.
But later,
Carlo realized he was alone
and had no place to go.

The sky began to get dark,
and the night air was cold.
Carlo didn't know what to do.
He needed a warm place to sleep.
He noticed an apartment with lights on.
Carlo scampered up the fire escape
and sprang through the open window
to check it out.

Carlo was certain that he had landed in one of those fancy hotels Mark's mother was always talking about. "Looks like I'll sleep here tonight," purred Carlo as he curled up on the soft, plush rug and fell asleep.

The next morning Carlo was startled by a shrill voice.
It came from a woman in a very pink dress.
"Oh, you're so cute!" she said.  "Lisa, look what I found!"
Lisa had always wanted to have a cat.
"I'll bring him some milk," she said excitedly.
"Good idea," said Lisa's Aunt Rose.
"In the meantime, I'll give him a bath."
Before Carlo knew what was happening, he was soaking
   in bubbles and smelling like a rose garden.

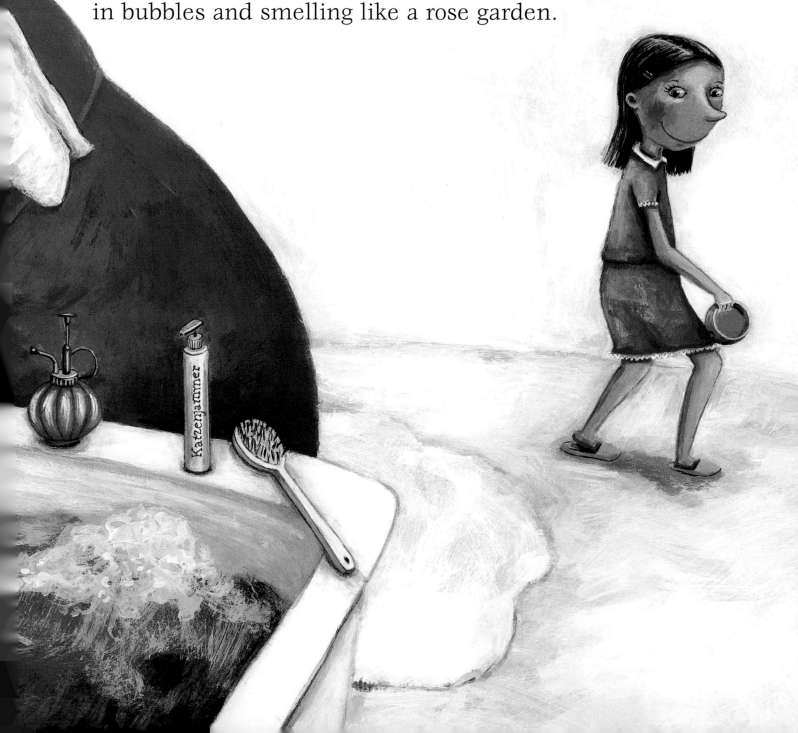

After Carlo's bath, Aunt Rose put him in a luxurious bed.
Every few hours Lisa fed him warm milk and expensive
treats. Carlo felt like a king.

"I've always dreamed of a life like this!"
he purred.

Between snacks Carlo
slept in his beautiful
bed or napped on
the satin sofa with Lisa.

Aunt Rose's house was so orderly that there
was nothing else for him to do.

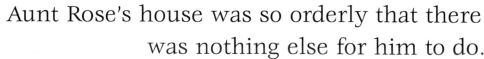

Carlo had found the good life! But as wonderful as it was,
he started to get bored with sleeping the whole day.
And those delicious snacks…
Well, they all began to taste the same.
"What I wouldn't give for a half-empty yogurt carton to
lick clean or a pile of dirty socks to snoop through!"
thought Carlo.

When Mark realized that Carlo was gone, he felt sad and lonely.

"Where do you think he is?" Mark cried. "What if something terrible has happened to him?"

"Don't worry," said Mark's father. "He'll come back eventually."

"I'm not so sure about that," said Mark's mother. "Who would want to live in a room as messy as yours?"

That night Mark couldn't sleep.

The next morning Mark hung a sign on his door
that said, "DO NOT ENTER!"
He watered his cactus plant, picked up his toys,
and hung up all his clothes.
Then Mark vacuumed his room and even took out
his trash.

When Mark took the sign down and let his parents in, his mother was shocked. "I don't believe my eyes!" she said. "Your room has never been so clean!"

"Do you think Carlo will like it?" Mark asked.
He filled Carlo's bowls with fresh food and
milk, then opened his window and waited.

It didn't take Carlo long to decide that he wasn't cut out
for the fancy life at Aunt Rose's. As soon as Carlo
thought that no one was looking, he snuck out the same
way he had gotten in.

When Carlo appeared at the window, Mark was delighted.
"You came back! What do you think of our room?"
Mark asked proudly. Carlo purred cheerfully.
He was happy to be home.
But as they cuddled up together
on Mark's bed, there was
a knock at the window.

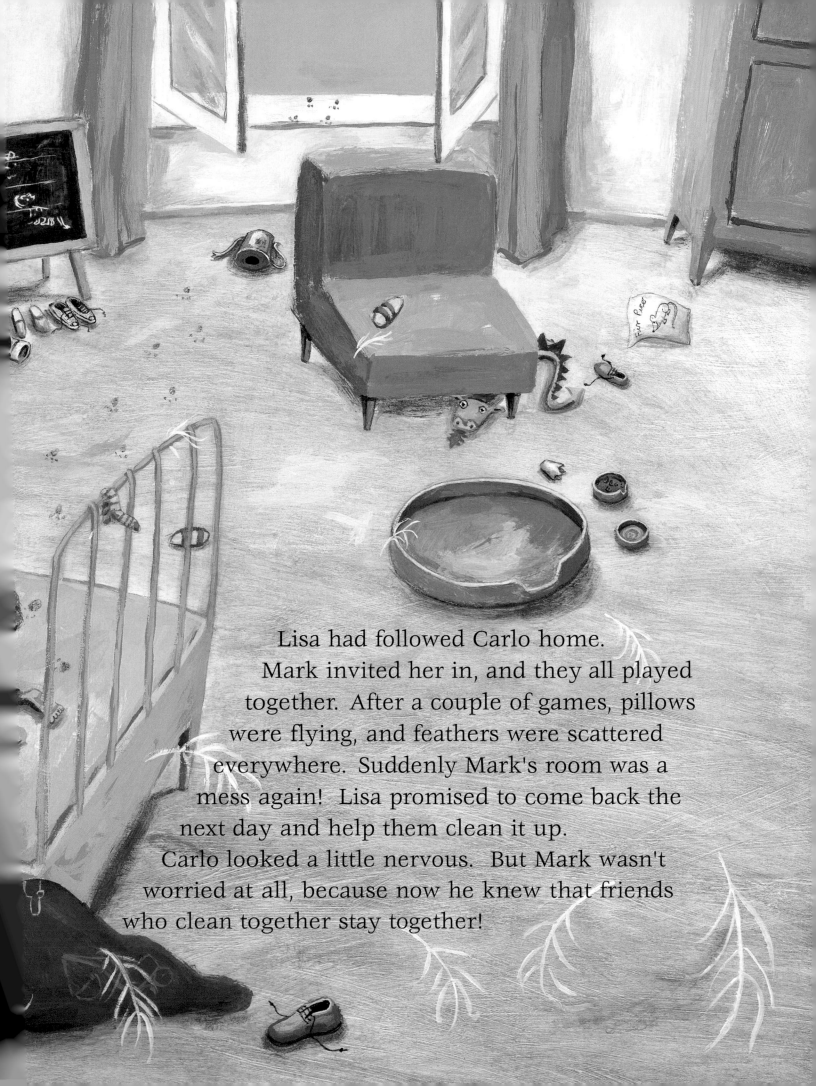

Lisa had followed Carlo home.
Mark invited her in, and they all played together. After a couple of games, pillows were flying, and feathers were scattered everywhere. Suddenly Mark's room was a mess again! Lisa promised to come back the next day and help them clean it up.
Carlo looked a little nervous. But Mark wasn't worried at all, because now he knew that friends who clean together stay together!

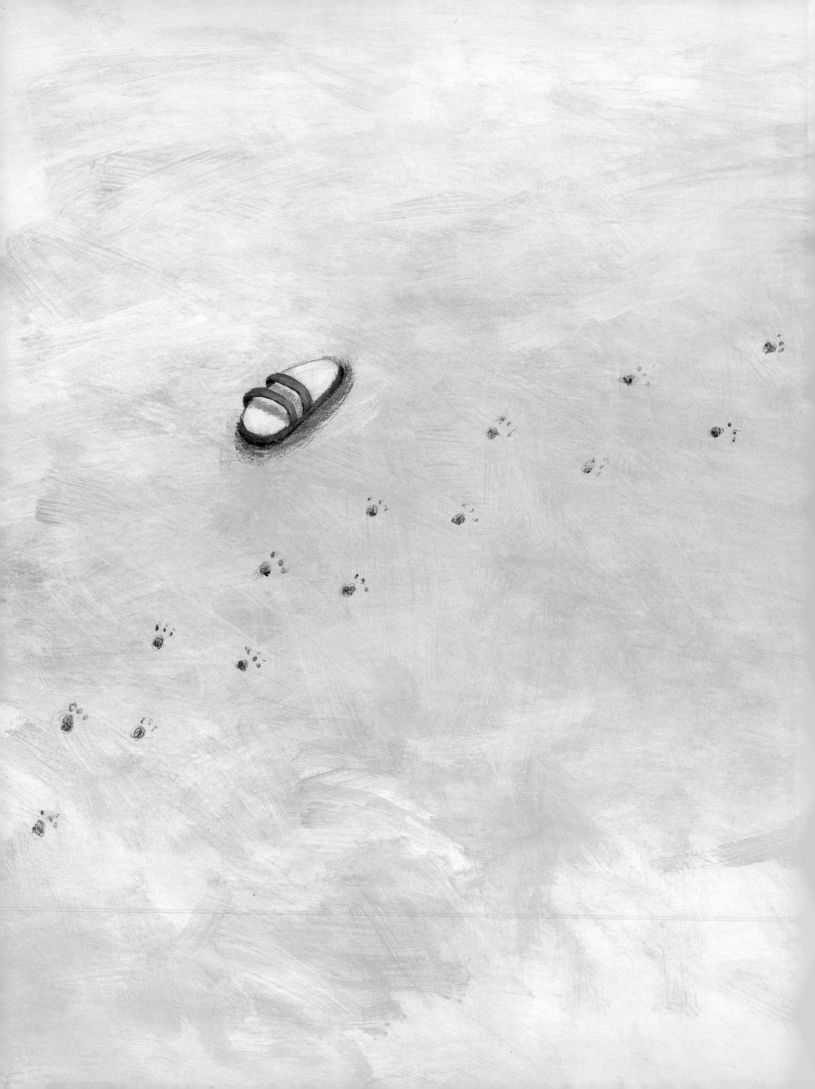